Animal Engineers

BEAVER DAMS

by Nancy Furstinger

FOCUS READERS

FOCUS READERS

www.focusreaders.com

Focus Readers is distributed by North Star Editions:
sales@northstareditions.com | 888-417-0195

Produced for Focus Readers by Red Line Editorial.

Photographs ©: Chase Dekker/Shutterstock Images, cover, 1; Puleo/iStockphoto, 4–5; Kerry Hargrove/Shutterstock Images, 7; DeniseBush/iStockphoto, 8–9; stanley45/iStockphoto, 10; Chris Moody/Shutterstock Images, 12; Teacherdad48/iStockphoto, 14–15; Holcy/iStockphoto, 16–17; Michel Loiselle/Shutterstock Images, 18, 29; LesPalenik/Shutterstock Images, 21; Photopictures/Shutterstock Images, 22–23; Josef Pittner/Shutterstock Images, 25; DaydreamsGirl/iStockphoto, 26

ISBN
978-1-63517-857-9 (hardcover)
978-1-63517-958-3 (paperback)
978-1-64185-161-9 (ebook pdf)
978-1-64185-060-5 (hosted ebook)

Library of Congress Control Number: 2018931107

Printed in the United States of America
Mankato, MN
May, 2018

About the Author

Nancy Furstinger is the author of more than 100 books. She has been a feature writer for a daily newspaper, a managing editor of trade and consumer magazines, and an editor at children's book publishing houses. She lives in upstate New York with a menagerie of animals.

TABLE OF CONTENTS

CHAPTER 1

BUSY BEAVER

A sleek, brown head pops out of the stream. It belongs to an American beaver. The large **rodent** swims to the shore. Then he waddles to a willow tree.

Beavers can hold their breath underwater for as long as 15 minutes.

The beaver uses his **incisors** to chew on the tree. Soon, the tree crashes to the ground. The beaver carries the heavy log through the water. He's building a dam.

The dam is made of rocks, logs, branches, and mud. These materials stop the flow of the

FUN FACT

Beavers have clear eyelids that serve as goggles. They help beavers see underwater.

Beavers' teeth contain iron, which helps them chew through trees.

stream. The beaver's hard work will result in a large, still pond.

CHAPTER 2

BUILDING A DAM

Beaver families work together to build dams. First, they find a low-lying spot where the water is not deep. They often choose streams with slow-flowing water.

A combination of logs, mud, and other material makes dams very strong.

Beavers must stay out of the way of falling trees. Otherwise, they can be crushed.

Next, the beavers build a **foundation**. They use their sharp front teeth to take down nearby trees. A beaver can chew through a small tree in only three minutes. However, larger trees take more time. After the tree falls, the beaver floats or drags it to the dam. Then it pushes the log deep into the mud.

FUN FACT

When beavers hear running water, they know their dam has a leak. They work quickly on repairs.

A beaver carries a tree branch to add to its dam.

The beavers use rocks or stumps to **anchor** the dam. After that, they add layers of logs and branches.

Lastly, they seal the dam using mud and plants. This keeps water from passing through.

Beavers keep busy. As a pond's water level rises, beavers make their dams larger. The average dam reaches 6 feet (1.8 m) high and 15 feet (4.5 m) long.

FUN FACT

The world's largest beaver dam is in Canada. It is twice as long as the human-made Hoover Dam.

A CLOSER LOOK

BEAVER DAM ENGINEERING

Like all engineers, beavers use math skills. But beavers don't use numbers. They use their **instincts**. For example, beavers make decisions based on the speed of water. If the **current** is moving quickly, they build a curved dam. This strengthens the dam.

A triangle shape gives the dam more protection. Beavers make the base of the dam wider than the top. Then, they slant the top toward the current. This helps the dam resist the force of the water.

Beavers built a curved dam at Grand Teton National Park.

CHAPTER 3

HOME SWEET HOME

Beaver families build dams to make ponds. Inside the pond, the beavers build a lodge. The lodge is where the adult beavers live with their babies. Baby beavers are called kits.

Lodges keep beavers safe and warm.

Beaver families keep to themselves while working.

Beaver lodges are dome-shaped structures with underwater entrances. Some lodges can be

10 feet (3.0 m) tall. The water around the lodge protects the beavers. It acts as a barrier from predators such as bears.

Dams result in deep, still water. These two features are important for building a lodge. Still water keeps the lodge from washing away.

FUN FACT

Other than humans, beavers change their environment more than nearly any other animal.

And deep water provides a place for storing food. Beavers prepare a supply of branches to eat during winter.

Sometimes, a beaver family builds more than one dam. This makes the pond deeper. Deep water is especially important in the winter. Beavers make sure their ponds are at least 4 feet (1.2 m) deep. That way, the entrances to their lodge do not freeze. And the beavers can still access their food.

Beaver lodges have small vent holes in the roof.

CHAPTER 4

A NEW HABITAT

Beavers create a new **habitat** when they build dams. These structures cause water to flood fields and forests. The resulting pond is a freshwater wetland. It becomes a home for other living things.

Since 1900, half of Earth's wetlands have disappeared. Beavers help save these habitats.

Many animals live in or near wetlands. Some are in danger of **extinction**. In North America, nearly half of at-risk species depend on wetlands.

More common animals rely on wetlands, too. Waterbirds rest on ponds during **migration**. Ducks

FUN FACT

Thousands of years ago, giant beavers roamed Earth. These beavers could grow up to 220 pounds (100 kg).

A Canada goose rests on a beaver dam during migration.

build nests on top of beaver lodges. Living within the pond are fish, turtles, and frogs. These animals attract predators such as herons and raccoons.

An elk finds food alongside a beaver dam.

Wetlands provide food for many other animals, too. Plants grow where beavers cut down trees. The plants then become food for deer and elk. When water levels rise, trees die. Insects feed on the dead trees. Then woodpeckers make a meal of the insects.

Wetlands also help humans. By keeping water on land, wetlands decrease the effect of **droughts**. Wetlands also take in water from floods. Wetlands even filter out toxins in water. This makes the water safer and cleaner for humans.

FOCUS ON

BEAVER DAMS

Write your answers on a separate piece of paper.

1. Write one sentence describing the purpose of beaver dams.
2. What type of wetland animal would you most like to see near a beaver dam? Why?
3. Where do beavers live?
    - A. lodges
    - B. kits
    - C. dams
4. What might happen if beavers stopped building dams?
    - A. Water in streams would be cleaner.
    - B. Wetland animals would have more food.
    - C. Droughts would be worse.

5. What does **seal** mean in this book?

*Lastly, they **seal** the dam using mud and plants. This keeps water from passing through.*

A. to decorate
B. to close gaps
C. to make hidden

6. What does **toxins** mean in this book?

*Wetlands even filter out **toxins** in water. This makes the water safer and cleaner for humans.*

A. poisonous matter
B. healthy plants
C. dangerous insects

Answer key on page 32.

GLOSSARY

anchor
To weigh something down or hold it in place.

current
The motion of a flowing waterway.

droughts
Periods of dry weather.

extinction
The process of an entire species dying out.

foundation
The supporting base of a structure.

habitat
The type of place where plants or animals normally grow or live.

incisors
Sharp front teeth used for cutting.

instincts
Behaviors that are natural instead of learned.

migration
When animals move to a different location, usually as the seasons change.

rodent
A small mammal that has sharp front teeth.

TO LEARN MORE

BOOKS

Borgert-Spaniol, Megan. *American Beavers.* Minneapolis: Bellwether Media, 2016.

Jennings, Dorothy. *How Do Beavers Make Dams?* New York: PowerKids Press, 2017.

Klepeis, Alicia Z. *American Beavers.* Mendota Heights, MN: Focus Readers, 2017.

NOTE TO EDUCATORS

Visit **www.focusreaders.com** to find lesson plans, activities, links, and other resources related to this title.

INDEX

Answer Key: 1. Answers will vary; **2.** Answers will vary; **3.** A; **4.** C; **5.** B; **6.** A